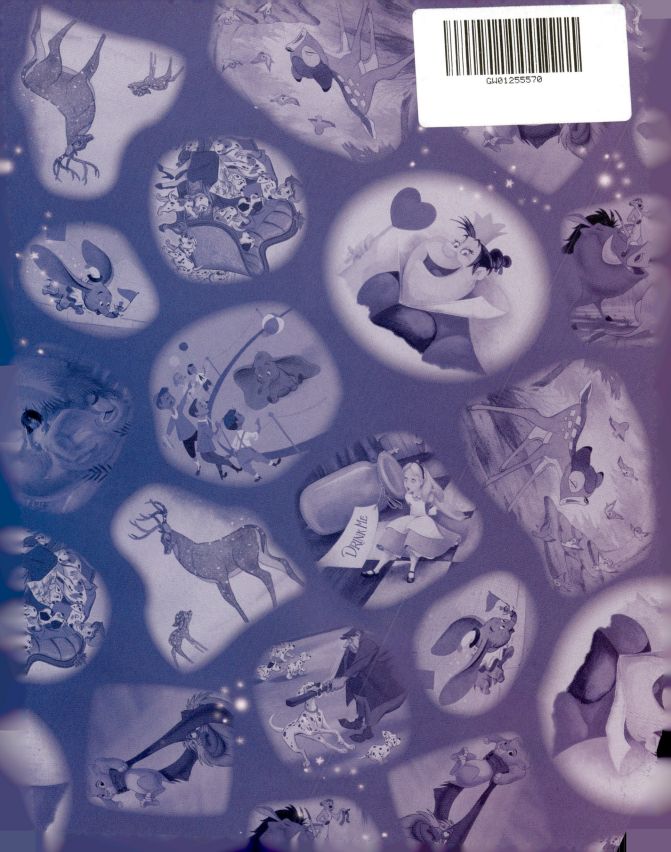

This book belongs to:

_____

Copyright © 2019 Disney Enterprises, Inc. All rights reserved.

Published by Scholastic Australia in 2019.

Scholastic Australia Pty Limited
PO Box 579 Gosford NSW 2250
ABN 11 000 614 577

www.scholastic.com.au

Part of the Scholastic Group
Sydney • Auckland • New York • Toronto • London • Mexico City • New Delhi
Hong Kong • Buenos Aires • Puerto Rico

All rights reserved. No part of this publication may be reproduced or transmitted in any form or by any means, electronic or mechanical, including photocopying, recording, storage in an information retrieval system, or otherwise, without the prior written permission of the publisher, unless specifically permitted under the Australian Copyright Act 1968 as amended.

ISBN 978-1-74383-243-1

Printed in China by RR Donnelley.

Scholastic Australia's policy, in association with RR Donnelley, is to use papers that are renewable and made efficiently from wood grown in responsibly managed forests, so as to minimise its environmental footprint.

10 9 8 7 6 5 4 3 2 1   19 20 21 22 23 / 1

CLASSICS

my favourite
Bedtime
storybook

SCHOLASTIC
SYDNEY AUCKLAND NEW YORK TORONTO LONDON MEXICO CITY
NEW DELHI HONG KONG BUENOS AIRES PUERTO RICO

Contents

Dumbo 5

Alice in Wonderland 17

The Jungle Book 29

Bambi 41

The Lion King 51

One Hundred and One Dalmatians . . . 63

Once there was a baby elephant named Dumbo. Dumbo's mother loved everything about him, but all the circus animals called him Dumbo because he had big, floppy ears.

Dumbo was proud to be part of the circus parade. But when he tripped over his BIG, FLOPPY EARS, everyone laughed at him. Poor Dumbo felt terrible.

Dumbo felt even worse when a group of boys made fun of him.

Dumbo's mother picked up one of the boys to stop him from harming her son. But the Ringmaster saw this and, fearing she was violent, took her away.

With Dumbo's mother gone, Timothy Q. Mouse felt sorry for the little elephant.

'I think your ears are BEAUTIFUL,' Timothy told him.

That is how Timothy and Dumbo became BEST FRIENDS.

But the other elephants didn't like Dumbo's big, floppy ears. Dumbo wasn't allowed to perform with them anymore. It made him SAD.

Dumbo didn't think he would ever fit in anywhere. He was too DIFFERENT.

One night, Dumbo dreamed he could FLY! Timothy told Dumbo that all he needed was to BELIEVE in himself and he could make the impossible come true. Dumbo trusted Timothy, so he believed in himself extra hard.

And that is how Dumbo became A FLYING ELEPHANT! Thanks to believing in himself, and a little bit of FRIENDSHIP, Dumbo became the most famous elephant in the world. He was also reunited with his mum.

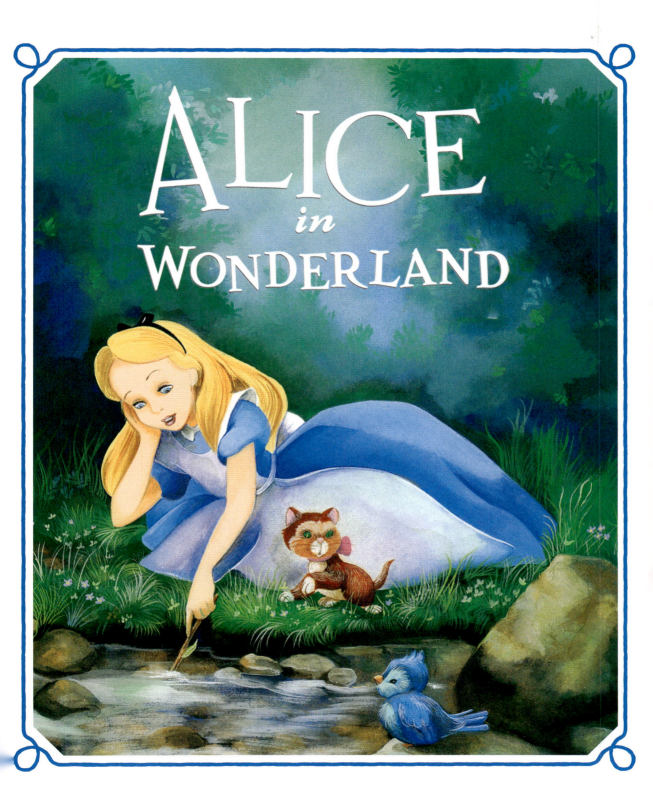

One day, a girl named Alice saw a white rabbit running by with a watch. He also spoke, and said that he was very late. Then he disappeared down a RABBIT HOLE.

Alice was a curious girl, so she followed him to WONDERLAND. There, nothing made much sense. For example, Alice drank a potion that made her very small!

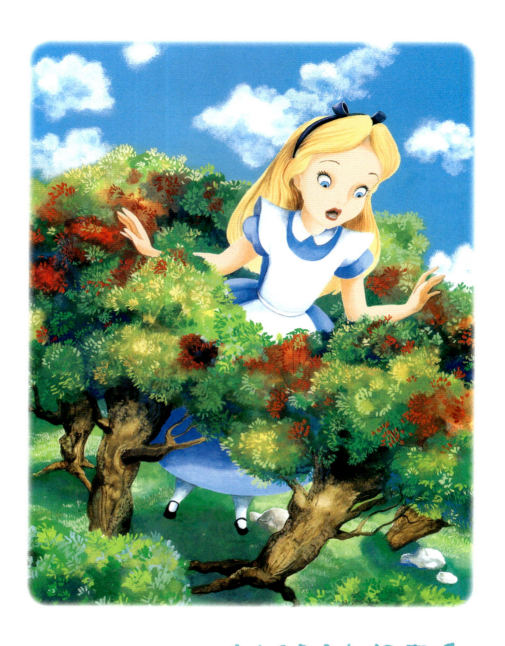

Later, she became VERY BIG.

TWEEDLEDEE and **TWEEDLEDUM,** two brothers who liked to recite poems, lived in Wonderland.

There was also a field of BEAUTIFUL FLOWERS. For a moment, Alice thought she heard a flower talk.

As she walked in Wonderland, Alice saw butterflies with bread for wings and a sleepy caterpillar who liked to recite poetry.

But Alice most wanted to see the White Rabbit. She was CURIOUS about what he was late for.

'If I were looking for a white rabbit,' said a CHESHIRE CAT, 'I'd ask the Mad Hatter.'

Then he disappeared.

Alice found the Mad Hatter. He was already with the White Rabbit!

'No wonder YOU'RE ALWAYS LATE. This watch is exactly two days slow,' the Mad Hatter told the White Rabbit, and popped open his watch.

The watch exploded and the White Rabbit fled.

Alice was upset. She had lost the White Rabbit again! But Alice still had more wonders to see—like the QUEEN OF HEARTS.

The Queen of Hearts had an army of cards at her beck and call. She also had quite the temper.

'OFF WITH HER HEAD!' the Queen yelled, pointing to Alice.

Alice thought she was doomed!

Just then, Alice heard a voice.

It was her sister!

Alice woke up and realised she was back at home. She decided that no matter how grown-up she became, she would always remember the

WONDERS OF WONDERLAND.

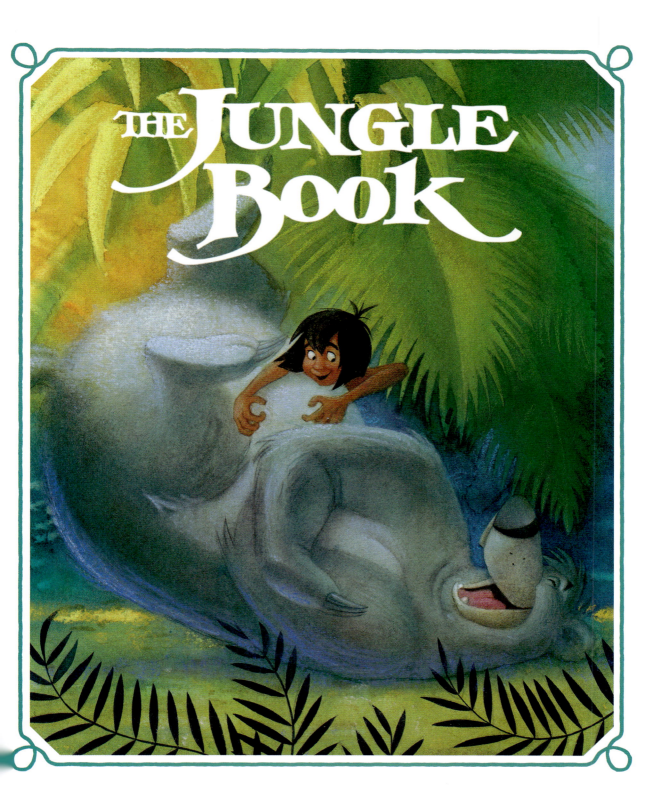

Long ago, in India, there was a boy named Mowgli. Mowgli wasn't like other boys: he lived in the jungle. And although Mowgli was **VERY HAPPY,** he never felt like he fit in.

Mowgli was raised by a pack of WOLVES. They liked how brave he was, like he was one of the cubs. But one day, the wolves learnt that a MEAN TIGER was coming, and they decided it would be safer for Mowgli if he left them.

The tiger's name was SHERE KHAN. Shere Khan didn't like humans—which meant he didn't like Mowgli.

A big panther named Bagheera loved and cared for Mowgli, just like the wolves had.

Bagheera thought the best place for Mowgli was OUT OF THE JUNGLE but Mowgli disagreed!

Bagheera wasn't being mean. He wanted what was best for Mowgli.

After the panther left, a snake named Kaa wanted to eat Mowgli!

Mowgli GOT AWAY, but he definitely didn't belong in the jungle with Kaa.

A bear named Baloo tried to teach Mowgli how to fight like a bear.

'Gimme a big bear growl,' Baloo told him.

'Grr!' Mowgli growled.

'No, no, no,' Baloo said. He wanted Mowgli to growl BIGGER!

Mowgli growled with all his might:

'GRRRRRR!'

But he wasn't the best bear.

Mowgli and Baloo laughed.

Mowgli wasn't the best ELEPHANT, either.

After all, he didn't have a trunk.

And Mowgli was a *terrible* monkey. The monkeys liked being mischievous and were always THROWING BREADFRUIT.

Mowgli was very lonely until he came across a group of vultures. But then the vultures used their wings to fly away!

Mowgli was alone until he spotted a strange creature. She lived in the Man-village by the river.

Mowgli was finally where he belonged.

All the forest animals gathered around a mama deer and her fawn. The fawn's name was BAMBI, and he was the new Prince of the Forest.

One day, Bambi noticed some creatures in the trees.
'Those are birds,' his friend Thumper explained.

'BIRD!' Bambi shouted.

The birds all flew away!

Then Thumper showed Bambi the FLOWERS.

'Flower!' Bambi said, this time more quietly.

'That's not a flower. That's a skunk!' Thumper giggled.

One morning, Bambi woke up to find that the world had turned white.

Bambi and Thumper had a lot of fun **ICE SKATING** at the pond. But Bambi still had much to learn.

In the winter, Man came and took Bambi's mother away.

His father, the Great Prince, would protect him now.

That was how Bambi learned about hope. He hoped that things would GET BETTER.

When he was older, Bambi fell in love with a BEAUTIFUL doe named Faline.

Bambi and Faline were very happy together. But then tragedy struck again: Man had set the forest on fire.

Bambi was not done learning, and that day he learned about FEAR.

From across the river, the forest animals watched as the fire destroyed their homes, but Bambi remembered an earlier lesson, and he did not give up hope.

When SPRING came around again, the forest was green. Bambi was now the Great Prince.

As he and his family began their lives together, Bambi thought of the lessons he wished to teach his children—and, most importantly, HOPE.

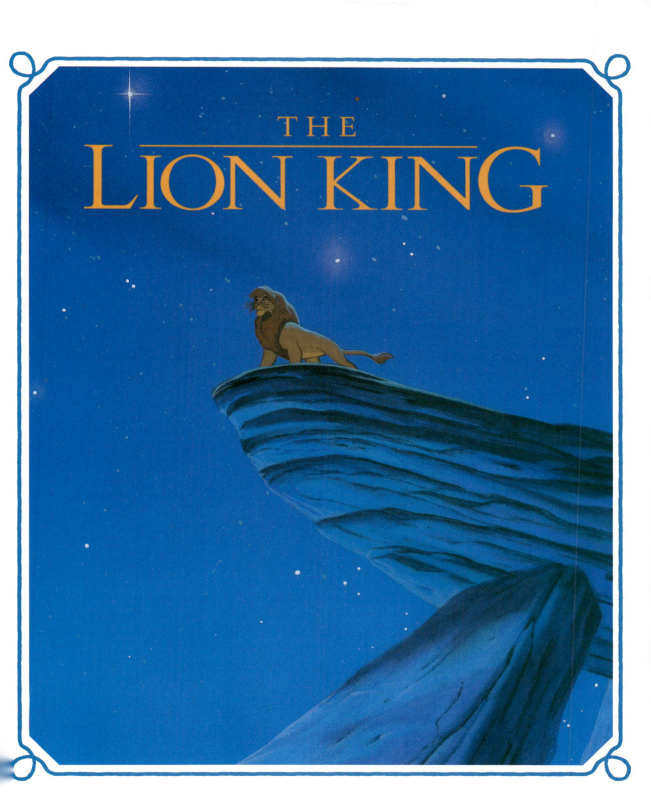

Mufasa was the king of a place called the Pride Lands. His son was named Simba and one day Simba would be KING.

But Scar, Mufasa's brother, wanted the kingdom all for himself. When Mufasa was in trouble, Scar did not help him but let him fall.

Simba believed his father's death was his fault, so he ran away. In his exile, Simba befriended a warthog named Pumbaa and a meerkat named Timon. They taught him something very important: **HAKUNA MATATA.** It means 'no worries'!

Simba grew up with that motto. One night, he, Timon and Pumbaa gazed up at the STARS.

Simba wondered if he had done the right thing by leaving the Pride Lands.

NALA was a lion who had been friends with Simba when they were young. One day, she found him.

Nala explained that as the new king, Scar had let the **HYENAS** take over the Pride Lands.

Simba was ashamed of himself. He told her that he didn't want to be king. Angry that Simba wouldn't help, Nala left.

Then Simba came across Rafiki, a baboon who lived in the Pride Lands.

Rafiki took Simba to a lake. There, Simba realised something. His father had been with him all along.

'YOU ARE MY SON AND THE ONE TRUE KING,' Mufasa reminded Simba. 'Remember who you are.'

Simba decided to go back to the Pride Lands.

In the PRIDE LANDS, Simba and Scar fought. Then Scar revealed a secret: he—not Simba—had killed Mufasa.

Simba knew what he had to do. He defeated Scar once and for all.

With Simba crowned as the **RIGHTFUL KING,** the Pride Lands returned to normal. Never again would Simba forget who he was.

But most importantly, the

CIRCLE OF LIFE

continued.

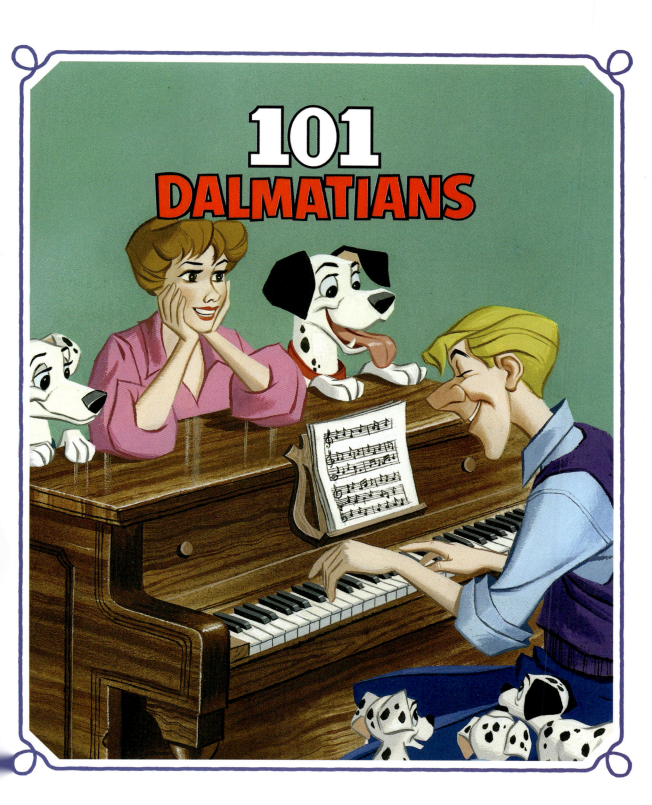

Once there was a litter of fifteen Dalmatian puppies. They lived in a small flat in London, but one day they went MISSING.

Their parents, PONGO and PERDITA, were desperate. They barked for help: 'Fifteen spotted puppies stolen. Have you seen them?'

The message reached a dog named the Colonel and a cat named Sergeant Tibs.

Tibs had heard puppies barking at the **DE VIL MANSION.**

'We'd better investigate,' said the Colonel.

Sure enough, the puppies were at the mansion. But it wasn't just the fifteen stolen puppies. There were NINETY-NINE puppies in all!

As soon as the news got back to Pongo and Perdita, they raced towards the mansion. It belonged to a woman named **CRUELLA DE VIL.**

Cruella wanted to make the puppies into a fur coat!

Pongo and Perdita distracted her henchmen while Tibs helped the puppies SNEAK out.

Then Pongo and Perdita decided to take all the puppies back to LONDON. The Dalmatians rolled in black soot to hide their spots so that Cruella wouldn't recognise them.

When the puppies returned to London, everyone was overjoyed. Their humans, Roger and Anita, decided to buy a place in the country.

'A HOME FOR DALMATIANS,' said Roger excitedly.

And that is exactly what they did!

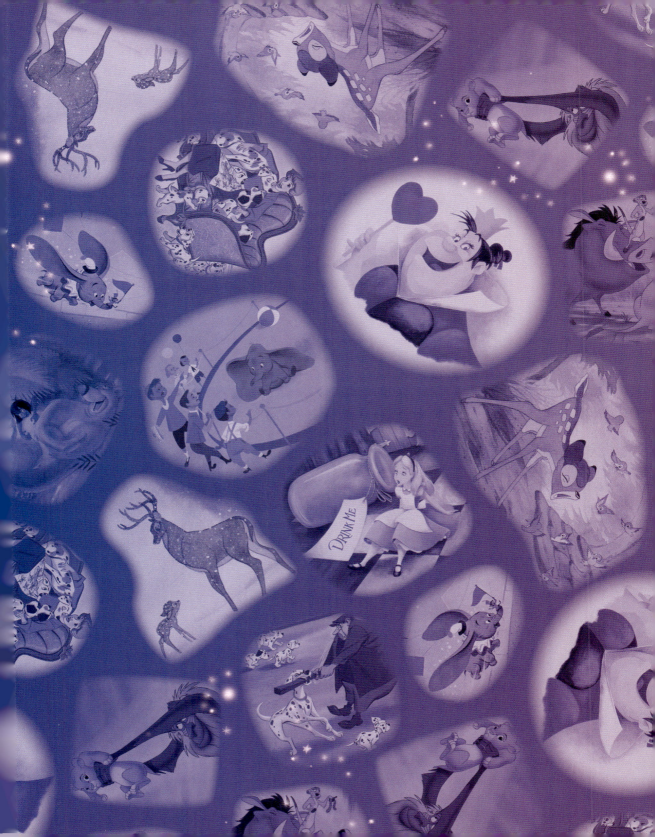